50¢

PUFFIN BOOKS

BALLET MAGIC

Harriet Castor grew up in Warwickshire, where she went to a full-time dancing school. She has been writing stories for as long as she can remember, and wrote her first Puffin book, *Fat Puss and Friends*, at the age of twelve. After graduating from Cambridge University with a degree in History, she lived in Prague for a while, teaching English and getting lost on trams. Returning to Britain, she spent the next few years as an editor in children's publishing, but now writes full-time.

D09973118

Some other books by Harriet Castor

FAT PUSS AND FRIENDS
FAT PUSS AND SLIMPUP
FAT PUSS ON WHEELS
MILLY OF THE ROVERS
MILLY'S GOLDEN GOAL

Harriet Castor
Ballet Magic

Illustrated by Chris Fisher

PUFFIN BOOKS

PUFFIN BOOKS

Published by the Penguin Group
Penguin Books Ltd, 80 Strand, London WC2R 0RL, England
Penguin Putnam Inc., 375 Hudson Street, New York, New York 10014, USA
Penguin Books Australia Ltd, 250 Camberwell Road, Camberwell, Victoria 3124, Australia
Penguin Books Canada Ltd, 10 Alcorn Avenue, Toronto, Ontario, Canada M4V 3B2
Penguin Books India (P) Ltd, 11 Community Centre, Panchsheel Park, New Delhi – 110 017, India
Penguin Books (NZ) Ltd, Cnr Rosedale and Airborne Roads, Albany, Auckland, New Zealand
Penguin Books (South Africa) (Pty) Ltd, 24 Sturdee Avenue, Rosebank 2196, South Africa

Penguin Books Ltd, Registered Offices: 80 Strand, London WC2R 0RL, England

www.penguin.com

First published 1999
3 5 7 9 10 8 6 4 2

Text copyright © Harriet Castor, 1999
Illustrations copyright © Chris Fisher, 1999
All rights reserved

The moral right of the author and illustrator has been asserted

Printed in Hong Kong by Midas Printing Ltd

British Library Cataloguing in Publication Data
A CIP catalogue record for this book is available from the British Library

ISBN 0–140–38479–0

"**B**allet?" said Jess, looking at the poster and then at her friend Flo. "Do I look like a ballerina to you?"

"Oh, please come with me," said Flo. "I've been wanting to start ballet lessons for ages. It'll be fun."

Jess frowned. "You know who'll be there, though, don't you? Primrose Pettifer."

Primrose Pettifer was in Jess and Flo's class at school. She was the nastiest, most stuck-up girl they knew. And she loved showing off. Ballet lessons would be too good a chance for Primrose to miss.

Still, Flo was Jess's best friend, so at last Jess said, "All right. I'll come with you to the first class –

just to keep you company. But you'll
have to go on your own after that.
Ballet isn't *my* idea of fun."

Flo grinned. "Thanks, Jess," she said.

The next Friday, after school, Jess
and Flo went to the Broad Street
Community Centre to join the new
ballet class.

Neither of them had proper ballet outfits; they just wore shorts and T-shirts, and took their shoes and socks off. Most of the other children there had done the same. But not –

"Primrose Pettifer!" hissed Flo. "Look!"

Primrose was wearing a pink tutu. She had pink tights on and proper pink ballet shoes with criss-crossed ribbons. Her hair was scraped into a bun, and she had even stuck pink flowers in it.

"Wow!" said Flo.

"I feel sick," said Jess. "I *knew* I shouldn't have come."

Jess and Flo and the other pupils went into the hall.

At first they thought it was
empty. But then suddenly – "Hello
everyone!" – two white-haired ladies
appeared, smiling sparkly smiles.

"I'm Miss Angelica Twirl," said the tall, thin lady.

"And I'm her sister, Miss Ethel Twirl," said the smaller lady, who was shaped a bit like a pudding.

Miss Ethel sat down at the piano. Miss Angelica clapped her

hands and asked everyone to spread
out. Jess, to her dismay, was made
to stand at the front. And then the
class began.

Miss Angelica taught everyone to
stand in 'first position', and do knee
bends, and point their feet, and

wave their arms about in a special way. She said there were five positions of the feet to learn, and five positions of the arms too, and Jess wondered how anyone ever remembered them all.

Then they did some jumping and skipping steps, which Jess liked best.

In fact, Jess was surprised to discover that she was enjoying herself. The Miss Twirls were very nice – though there seemed to be something a little odd about them. Jess wasn't quite sure what it was.

Miss Angelica showed the class how to point their feet when they jumped. She jumped into the air herself, and was so busy explaining . . .

... that she stayed there!

Jess stared. She thought her eyes were going to pop out of her head.

"Oh, silly me!" said Miss Angelica, turning bright red and

coming back to earth with a bump. "That step was far too tricky for beginners."

Wow! thought Jess. Now *that* would be a good step to learn!

A minute later, Miss Angelica and Miss Ethel had an argument. It was about the music. Miss Ethel thought it should go quite slowly, so everyone had time to jump nice and high. Miss Angelica thought it should go faster, so they could do small, quick jumps. Miss Ethel lost the argument. She pulled a very cross face.

"Ethel!" hissed Miss Angelica sternly. "Behave yourself!"

But when Miss Angelica turned her back, Jess heard Miss Ethel

mutter something. And the next
moment, Jess saw that Miss
Angelica's hair bun had turned into
a real bun – with currants in it!

Jess was amazed. It looked very
funny. She had to suck in her
cheeks hard to stop herself from
giggling. She turned round to see if
Flo was giggling too.

But Flo hadn't spotted the currant

bun. And neither had the other
children. Perhaps it's me, then,
thought Jess. Perhaps this is a dream.

She pinched herself. It hurt. She
rubbed her eyes. But the currant
bun was still there.

Not for long, though. After the next exercise, Miss Ethel wiggled her fingers. A moment later, the bun turned back into hair again. Jess stared at the Miss Twirls. What on earth, she wondered, was going on?

"Oh, I almost forgot!" said Miss Angelica at the end of the class. "If you decide to come to ballet every week, dears, you will need to buy some clothes and shoes. First you will need a leotard. I've brought one along to show you."

Miss Angelica turned round to rummage in her bag.

From her place at the front, Jess saw that she couldn't find what she was looking for. Then Miss Angelica clicked her fingers. In a puff of

smoke, a leotard appeared. Miss
Angelica turned back to the class as
if she had just found it. "Here it is!"
she said.

This time Jess didn't pinch herself
or rub her eyes. She stood quite still
and thought hard. She had had an
idea.

Meanwhile, Primrose Pettifer, who had been showing off all lesson, was saying loudly, "*I* don't need a leotard. Tutus are much better. This one was very expensive."

Miss Angelica shook her head. "Tutus are fine for an end-of-term

show, Primrose dear," she said.
"But for class you should wear a
leotard. After all, we don't wear our
party clothes every day, do we?"

"Obviously not," said Primrose
rudely, looking at Miss Angelica's
plain blouse and skirt.

Then Miss Angelica noticed
Primrose's ballet shoes. "Those
won't do at all," she said. "They're
far too big for your feet, dear. And
they're toe shoes, with hard ends.
You won't be able to dance on your
toes for several years yet, I'm
afraid."

"I shall if I like," said Primrose,
sticking her nose in the air.

"Then you'll hurt your feet and
never be a ballet dancer," said Miss

Angelica. "You must dance in bare feet, until your parents buy you some soft shoes that fit properly."

"Don't want any," said Primrose. "What use is a ballet class if I can't wear my tutu and my toe shoes?"

And she twinkled round on the spot with her arms in the air to show everyone how fine she looked.

Primrose was very rude. She was used to getting her own way. Jess noticed that Miss Ethel, at the piano, was looking cross.

"I shall wear them every lesson," Primrose went on. "Just try and stop me!"

Jess saw Miss Ethel fix Primrose with a funny look and then wink. Jess wondered if anything strange would happen this time. She turned round to see. No – Primrose looked just the same as usual. Jess frowned, puzzled.

But then after the class, when the

children were back in the changing-
room, strange things did start
happening to Primrose after all.

First she had trouble with her
shoe ribbons. The knots in them
didn't seem to want to come
undone.

"Stupid things!" muttered
Primrose crossly.

At last, she untied the ribbons

and stuffed the shoes into her bag.
But when she turned her back, Jess
saw something amazing.

There was a wriggling inside the
bag. The zip came open and Jess
saw the end of a pink ribbon
waving, like a little hand. Then
another appeared, and, slowly but

surely, Primrose's ballet shoes began to climb out, all by themselves!

Jess's mouth dropped wide open. Flo was just going to say something about catching flies when she spotted the ballet shoes too. They were slithering their way over the floor, making straight for Primrose.

Meanwhile, Primrose was struggling with her tutu. She couldn't get it off. It was sticking to her hands like candyfloss.

When she saw the shoes, Primrose forgot about her tutu. She shrieked and jumped on to a chair. The ballet shoes slithered after her, wrapping their ribbons around the chair legs. They were desperate to climb up, but couldn't manage it.

And Jess was certain that she could
hear faint whimpering noises.

"You've done this!" screeched

Primrose, pointing at Jess. "You've put mice in them! You've got them on strings!"

Everyone in the changing-room looked at Jess in amazement.

"It wasn't me!" said Jess, trying not to laugh.

But no one believed her.

Just then, the door to the hall
opened and Miss Ethel put her head
round it.

"Atishoo!" she sneezed. "Bless
me, dears!" She disappeared.

The shoes lay still. Cautiously,

Primrose climbed down from the chair. She prodded her tutu. It wasn't sticky any more.

Primrose glared at Jess. "I don't know what sort of joke you thought that was," she snapped. "But it wasn't funny!"

Jess took no notice. She grinned at Primrose. Now she was certain: she had solved the mystery.

"How did you do it, then?" asked Flo, when she and Jess were sitting on the wall outside the Community Centre, waiting for the bus.

"I didn't," said Jess. "It was Miss Ethel. You see . . ." Jess paused. "I think the Miss Twirls can do magic."

"Ha, ha, ha," laughed Flo. "Ha, ha – oh." Suddenly she stopped. Jess wasn't laughing. Jess really meant it. Flo's eyes grew round as saucers. "M-magic?" she said.

Jess nodded. Then she told Flo about all the strange things she had seen in the ballet class.

"And did you notice Miss Ethel sneeze just before Primrose's shoes and tutu went back to normal?" she added.

"Maybe Miss Ethel has a cold," said Flo. "But then again – wow! – maybe you're right."

"Yes," said a voice behind them.
"Maybe you are."

Jess and Flo turned their heads
so fast, they almost fell off the wall.
They found Primrose Pettifer
standing behind them.

"Two horrid old witches – I

should have known!" she said.
"No wonder they wouldn't let me
wear what I wanted." She thought
for a moment, and then a nasty
smile crept over her face. "But I
shall get my revenge!"

"What do you mean?" said Jess.

Just at that moment, a man
hurried past. It was Mr Wolf, who
was in charge of the Community
Centre and arranged all the classes
there.

"Mr Wolf! Mr Wolf!" Primrose
called, dashing after him. "I've
got something to tell you! It's
urgent! And it's very, very
important!"

Mr Wolf turned round. He
frowned at Primrose. "I'm busy

now," he said, flipping open his
computer diary. "But you can come
and see me . . ." He pressed some
buttons and peered at the tiny
screen. "Tomorrow," he said.
"Twelve o'clock sharp."

"I will," said Primrose. As Mr
Wolf hurried off, she turned to Jess
and Flo. "And that will be the end

of those beastly Miss Twirls! Mr
Wolf won't let witches take ballet
lessons. He'll find a proper teacher,
who lets me wear my tutu!"

After Primrose had gone home, Jess
and Flo were still sitting on the
wall. The bus was late.

"It's all my fault," said Jess.

"We've just discovered the most
exciting thing that's happened for
. . . for –"

"Years," said Flo. "Maybe *ever*."

"And now I've spoilt it!" Jess
wailed. "Mr Wolf will send the Miss
Twirls away."

There was a miserable silence.

Then Flo said, "We should warn

them. If they can do magic, perhaps they can stop Primrose."

Jess thought. Jess smiled. Then she said, "Brilliant idea, Flo!" and hugged her. "We must find out where they live," she added, "and go and see them as soon as we can."

Jess and Flo looked up the Miss Twirls in the telephone directory and wrote out their address. It wasn't far from Jess's house. So first thing the next morning, they made their way there.

The house had a brass knocker on the door in the shape of a ballerina. The curtains at the windows were red velvet, like stage curtains in a theatre. There was something special about the place, though it was hard to say exactly what. But the smoke that rose from the chimney seemed to curl and, well, *twirl* in a rather unusual way.

As they stared at the house, Jess and Flo heard someone coming.

"Quick!" whispered Jess. "Behind those plant pots!"

They saw Miss Angelica walking up the path. She was looking for something in her handbag.

"I bet she's forgotten her keys," whispered Flo.

Miss Angelica glanced up and down the street. Then, in a little puff of smoke, she disappeared.

"She's magicked herself inside!" hissed Jess. "Come on – let's ring the bell."

"But wait," said Flo. "What if they're only pretending to be nice – and really they're nasty witches like Primrose said? And, anyway, if they really could do magic they would know we were hiding here right now, wouldn't they?"

Just at that moment, a window opened behind them. Miss Ethel looked out. "You're right, Angelica," she called, "it's Jessica and Florence. Come in, dears, and have a cup of tea."

Jess and Flo looked at each other and gulped. Then they climbed out from behind the plant pots and went inside.

There was tea and lemonade, and there were lots of delicious biscuits, baked by Miss Ethel. At last, Jess plucked up the courage to ask her question.

"Oh no, dear, we're not witches!" laughed Miss Ethel. "You have to take exams for that –"

"And get proper certificates," added Miss Angelica.

"But we have a little something . . ." Miss Ethel wiggled her fingers.

Jess and Flo looked at one
another. "Then you might be in
trouble," said Jess. "Listen . . ."

And she told the Miss Twirls
about Primrose Pettifer and how she
was going to tell Mr Wolf
everything at twelve o'clock sharp.

"This is serious," said Miss
Angelica.

"Very serious indeed," said Miss
Ethel.

"Some people have a funny idea
about magic," said Miss Angelica.
"It comes from reading too many

fairy stories."

Miss Ethel nodded. "People pricking their fingers and going to sleep for a hundred years. What piffle!"

"There's only one thing for it,"
said Miss Angelica, putting on her
coat. "We'll have to stop Primrose!"

"Should we come too?" asked
Jess.

46

"Oh yes, dear, of course!" said Miss Ethel. "We're going to need your help."

At twelve o'clock sharp, Primrose Pettifer knocked on Mr Wolf's office door.

"Come in!" said Mr Wolf.

Outside the window, the bushes rustled. Jess, Flo and the Miss Twirls were hiding there.

"Is it her?" hissed Flo.

"I . . . can't . . . Yes. Yes, it's Primrose!" said Jess.

"Right," said Miss Angelica. "Ethel – do your stuff!"

Miss Ethel began making strange shapes with her hands. Her eyebrows twitched. Her chins trembled.

"Are you casting a spell?" asked Jess, who had been given a dandelion and been told to circle it clockwise.

"It's . . . a . . . very tricky . . . kind of . . . charm," said Miss Ethel. "A Charm Charm."

"What's that?" asked Flo, circling *her* dandelion anti-clockwise.

"It makes nasty people charming," explained Miss Angelica. "They can't say a single cross word. But it's very difficult to do. Concentrate, Ethel!"

"So, Primrose," Mr Wolf was

saying. "What was it you wanted to tell me?"

"I wanted to say . . ." began Primrose.

"Quickly, Ethel!" hissed Miss Angelica.

"I wanted to say that the Miss Twirls are . . ."

"Yes?" said Mr Wolf.

"Are awf– awfu–" stammered Primrose.

"Awful?" said Mr Wolf.

Primrose's face looked very odd, as if she was having trouble controlling her lips. "Are awfully nice," she finished at last. She scowled, and tried again. "They're rot– rot–"

"Rotten?" suggested Mr Wolf.

Primrose's lips wobbled. "They spoil us rotten!" she said.

"Well, you're very lucky then," said Mr Wolf, glancing impatiently at his watch.

"W– wi–" said Primrose, waving her hands desperately. "Witches!"

"Bother!" hissed Miss Ethel.

"Ethel! Do something!" hissed Miss Angelica.

Mr Wolf looked at Primrose. He thought for a moment. Then he frowned. He said, "Which is . . .? Which is . . .? Do spit it out, child! Which is *what*?"

"Which is why I like them so

much!" said Primrose, with the meanest look on her face that Jess had ever seen.

A minute later, Primrose was being ushered out of Mr Wolf's office. "I'm a very busy man," he was saying. "Perhaps the next time you want to tell me how much you like your ballet teachers, you could write me a letter, hmm?"

"Oh yes, th-thank you, Mr Wolf," said Primrose, shaking her head.

"Strange girl!" muttered Mr Wolf, and he went back into his office.

Once Primrose was safely out of sight, Jess, Flo and the Miss Twirls climbed out of the bushes and dusted themselves down.

"Phew!" said Miss Ethel, searching

for her handkerchief. "That was exhausting. I feel drained."

She did look rather tired.

"Will Primrose be like that for ever?" asked Jess hopefully.

Miss Ethel shook her head. "The Charm Charm will wear off in time," she said. "Luckily, though,

she won't remember anything about what's happened. She won't remember going to see Mr Wolf, or even wanting to. But she *will* go back to being the same old Primrose. So we'll have to keep an eye on her."

"We'll have to keep an eye on

you too!" said Miss Angelica sharply. "Dear me, Ethel, your temper gets us into such trouble! Think before you wink next time!"

Later, as Jess and Flo were walking home, Flo said, "If Primrose won't remember anything about the Charm Charm, do you think she'll come to ballet next week in her tutu and toe shoes again?"

"And if she does, will Miss Ethel be able to keep her temper?" laughed Jess. "I can't wait to see!"

Flo frowned. "But Jess – you said you would only come to the first ballet lesson, and never again after that."

"Did I?" said Jess. "Well, I've changed my mind. Ballet has turned out to be much more fun than I expected."

"Ballet's great, it's ace, it's cool . . ." said Flo, spinning like a ballerina down the street.

"In fact, you know what?" Jess giggled. "I think it's magic!"